Vicinities

Also by Lisa Lubasch:

How Many More of Them Are You?

Vicinities

Lisa Lubasch

Avec Books
Penngrove

I am grateful to the editors of the following publications in which some of these poems first appeared, occasionally in different form: *Boulevard, Denver Quarterly, New American Writing, Jacket, Seneca Review, American Letters & Commentary, Verse, Volt, Fence, First Intensity, Fourteen Hills, The Hat, Cello Entry, Near South, The Portable Boog Reader,* and *can we have our ball back?*

I also thank Jill Stengel for publishing part of this collection in her a+bend press chapbook series. L.L.

ISBN: 1-880713-27-6

Library of Congress Control Number: 2001012345

Cover art by Louise Bourgeois:
Front cover *Untitled* (recto), 1993; gouache and pink ink on blue paper; 14-1/2 x 23-1/8"; 36.8 x 58.7 cm.
Back Cover: *Untitled* (verso), 1993; gouache and pink ink on blue paper; 14-1/2 x 23-1/8"; 36.8 x 58.7 cm.
Courtesy of Cheim & Read, New York
Photo: Zindman Fremont

Cover design by Colleen Barclay

First Edition

Avec Books
P.O. Box 1059
Penngrove, CA 94951

for Max

CONTENTS

with your fingers tensed lengthening and quaking
            like eyes
the flame summons to grip

—Tristan Tzara

GROUND SWAYS

I pale away. The birds slick up.
Each of their lives is gathered in miniature.
All partings are this disappearance.
Things veer off. And each of us.

I

ONCE

BEYOND EACH PREFACE

beyond each preface
a scattering and
an island of
intransigence
where you rest
and read and roam
in that loom
of least knowing
lost to an ever-folding
hour you pull back—
from your mouth
words incongruous
with the night
that enters them—
feared not less
for plummeting
into
plain dust
and a wall of irises

ONCE

and then
only, if the way
was wrong,
the way
divulging itself,
you peered out
from rain, late
rain re-
tracing
buried sun.

THAT ALL WITHIN ME LIES

that all within me lies
in lowing over it

even this dark mist
surrounding
my own pallid reflection

how it wants to lose itself

to dark and
be quickly
dispensed with—

is it me
exacting a return?

more than this allows
I miss

blind, vertiginous
hands, furled
numbers for

all this time

the day
like speech
covering its openings

indecency of
rain
running edgelessly

over the field, farther fields rather
fold, far off
lowing or undone

and
gone—

arrive again silently
possible solace

            everything
its own voiceless admission
sealing itself

(cannot seal itself)

one long utterance left—

SHE LAUGHS

she laughs
as if to distinguish
the breach
from the breach
the bold laugh
under now
forgetting
(time)

WHEN I WALK

when I walk I understand
that between me
the air my hands
reaching down
to define
ground
a memory—
how can you
be
if I
though
how
it was
it was ever

EVEN A DAY

if left to spring's
injunctions

my one lost
purpose

even a day

---

furtive day
fields
undoing themselves
in what I—

each strand
again
stranded the day
in its generosity
opens outward a cloud
researched
to the point of forgetting

and if I offer you
this if I give
to you this
truly
uncentered
hope
not as an ending
neither opening nor

II

VICINITIES

ASCENT

Neither here nor in peripheral light

Yellow in the gruesome forest

Not hearing leaves grown tangled besides

We find our gods on the wet-blown grass

Blowing in the door blowing in

*

That desire came consistently and without rain,
the unstifled blew in the door to relieve us, "we were just
that way," always arriving
neither here nor there,
frightening ourselves. Meanwhile I kept writing
these lyrics that wouldn't take,
and the blue light grew into
fall. Isn't this
my eclogue after all?

*

Reciting our pledges,
asking the waiter to bring us some tea
and a samovar, an early tonic . . .

We lost all sense of follow-through—
pursuer, pursued—we couldn't keep up, though we'd be tempted
to try, given the locus of desire we'd uncovered

in our boots. The shoots had already detangled
and dried, the blown azaleas were waiting.
What was stopping us? Could it be

some silly protocol? The gross insistence
that could never be had
enough . . .

*

Then the sound was wrong, wrung out
in starts and bangs—

Something was said at the start
I can't remember, the marred sense of it
strayed through the door

and fell silent, somewhere in the middle . . .

What I think it had to do with was
those ghost-like few that led us home
when we should have been going to the dance,

although for now, the turn-round was enjoyable,
revelatory, something akin to our desire for light
inside the rain.

*

Spring was approaching, the tired hinge
of visors getting closer
then receding into leaves . . .

It was a time of

festivals in tents and smallish rites—
and the high bramble you pulled upward,
and some roughly few vices

in the bayberry bush.

*

No matter. Those who spent the day in other ways
knew something different from us,
something perhaps a little more abstract

though hardly vocable—the candied kid-light
that suddenly grew . . .

When you
became *you* no longer,
you were nowhere to be found—

but the fixed idea or motion of
that phantasm still grew beyond the clouds,
something to define us by,

no matter how briefly.

*

Displeased with our new habit
of returning,
we made our beds and

felt a sense of

how gruesome the first time you were kissed by it
felt—the clod-heeled myopic sensation
of pain,

its wriggled punishment.

*

(and already the night's long fog
unfolding in the most predictable way—
but then, there will be time

to throw ourselves into something
dark and faithless, time

to be swallowed up by vicinity—)

ENOUGH TO SAY

. . . but there was the larger pattern
of the fall to keep in mind. A saddish contempt for
getting things wrong.
The tritones kept us happy, or enamored
with the prospect of new pain, another
resolve. All through the broken lines,
you went to my heart . . .

The saying we knew
to fall from (the way everything fell
when it was time)—were we the only ones it didn't notice, account for, take
into account? I love you in a language we've agreed to keep
quiet about. In a diligent refusal of what's ours.

JUST THE SAME

That our progress resembled a climate.
                    Our sins brought to mind,
inside the walls. I would send for them
only when they were due . . .

                                        But the god refused us

(and the cinch or the tether—that grew all by itself
around those walls and symbolized the same course of events.)

IN RAIN OUT OF LIGHT

When the bride was spoken for, the narrative ensued. Arose out of a copse.

No one recognized it, deep as rivers.

In the rain, a procession of men.

In the rain, spiked woods lashed in the distance.

Noise of shadows.

III

AGAINST THE HOURS

"To stay here only to have. To protect one from the inhabiting low."

Not having heard that, the voice pushes back, "We should get ready to go—"

Start here. Personages abound. Dash to perform. Unbounded I. Then—a turncoat blushes like a key descendant of the trained administration. O, pernicious vowel. You are consumed by a mere brightness!

To mark death. *From here to death.* In the leaves ran the child. She was happy to see the spirit of death in the trees. There were others there too, in the leaves, near death. A wind blew out. Death's mouth.

(A MORPHOLOGY OF LIGHT)

*

glomming on to us in the low
still heat, the low

Etruscan light,—
stammering, thin-eyed

hermetic child,—

can *you* define beauty for me?
can you?

*

(the mute incipient soul
of death's mailed hand)

*

the slow cumbersome looting of the soul (through light)

*

(a freakish lump in the ambrosiac dawn)

laid into a vacancy

*

“if we change places, and I low up for dark—”

*

drawn to the nearest weld-light, leaf-light—

your eyes. dear typhous lilies   fallen.

What folly do I fit?
(There's the fish. You're the kingfisher. Catch it!)

Alas, my fate requires that I give it back.

Foul Eternity. Swindling the grave.

THE LURE OF GRAVITY

"There stands the life." And here stands the lowered consciousness . . .

With each bandaged, desultory breath

That which renders me "in life." A falsification seeking and retrieving itself . . .

"I am alone here." The first lie . . .

Shrug of spring—a hoax.

My scowl in your eye.

(A MORPHOLOGY OF TIME)

Meanwhile,

sleep, the eternal
withdrew—

what you are
the end of

doors,   slow-latched.

A hand on its mutable entrance—

IV

NEAR

". . . O yonder that incessant bloom—that makes the fallen look more fallen."

FIRST MEMORY OF IMPERMANENCE

Floats past us
in waves, gradually
replaced by
what failed light,
you turn away, toward

the heart's
haggard rim, rough, gleams,
blurring
now,
and the leaves, folding.

(A MORPHOLOGY OF FORGETTING)

*

between obstructed
(adequate)

slop-growth in the garden
veering

fear gave out

the unleased house
dissolute turnkey
hung deviate rot

*

Forget

the displaced figures, withdrawals—
whatever without light survives
the lighted

and the revulsion of re-
entering

*

the real
fell off

Into the dark
castabout, hung   Turned low in the light
Castaway, clung to   spiked   clump of stems
Scouring   and dripping

Blowing curses at the wind,
You might as well smoke it
outward now
Into

This lateral forest   Havocked
Erase   This threshold

APPARITIONS

*

What I devour in myself, what I lean towards devouring—the seed of that auspicious dream.

*

the slow-heeded margin of what seems

grieving   *my stilled heart*

*

And was deafened. Deadened. Unwieldy in the opened forest. Was unable to grow eyes . . .

*

"Today, there is a feeling of unhope, and the whole world chances to greet it."

To neither sanctify it nor to look upon it.

(brutality, contradiction)
twinned into the darkness

AGAINST THE HOURS

*

Stirring in a miasmic dawn . . .
The kneed sleeper is restless.

*

To stir, inconsequentially. And not to define, entirely, that movement whereby evil is a substitute for evil.

*

Writhing to awaken eventually becomes an Art of Life.

INSCRIBED IN AIR

Her hands were rotten. Across the slope of woods, a spired noon arose

*

A spiteful knowing arises in my glands. Must I make what's mutable my own?

*

You will not answer

*

Only a long and tired silence would loose her from the world,

a long and quiet flight   from the stir of dawn

---

in the breath of this stone—

a word, in my loneliness
taking of the name
one line
(less)

SWEPT IN

Now to unsay her, now to reenter
her inside the open door

                    at the door, in the room
with a dog-mane on—
                    In whose eyes a werewolf came
to beseech her now come home—

(A MORPHOLOGY OF GRAMMAR)

*

Slow divisive   incinerate

anchor indeterminate

black transfer

*

the mast forsaken. O
betoken loneliness.

*

monstrous and profligate

garnering a misery

---

the ruinous demarcation dark

effluvial den

*

As through some thick expanse of sound, I

let these fall

*

fury into words

*

the lonely fundamental that precedes us—

*

Dire—
this dress of yore
wherefore I willingly
accede—

torn
lashing out, in turn

*

that "I" is not response to but unraveled for

The atrocity of Mind

(A reprieve of this set of passions   inference, oneliness, law,   rages against Idea)

(the moldering pause)

(the attraction

to the fissures of

the retracted

line)

(ON MATTER AND THE PRINCIPAL SYSTEMS OF WORLDS)

*

a lighted ardent vestibule of sound and elision of
signs, cast-off—
crumbling shapes pulled under a circumference.

*

And here, the eclosion of forms
willed hollow,—

the many one
names.

*

mocked-up across distances
you carefully run your fingers down-

fisted and howling
all the thankless bitterment of stars, cragged

in the deep-felled,

cramped moonlight.

*

(this lightness into which everything implores itself—)
(transfigured, low
involute light)

V

THE REFUSAL

THE REFUSAL

(1)

Even then, what looked like just a series
of unpleasant starts was something else entirely,
something impossible to say,
or why in the threadlight (there) the season took root.
You were depressed then, coming in last
from the rain. You made it home
without too much heavy clatter, but the (   ) that streaked the windows
rang the bells.

Just the same,
the lunatics are bored, though the fed and scarred
mouth of the forest continues to grow.

The latest news flash has me all keyed up
for the distance, which, once permissive, is now withdrawing
at warp speed across the providential

tow of (   ) that I feel as my own
hoarse utterance—the dull vox of the eternal
trying to work itself out, somehow, in tandem

with the rest. It makes sense
for now. Until the universal I hear as a moan
drowns out point of view.

                                        Or is it the other way around?
The giant landscape rising to be seen.

I'm not convinced. Some bit of statuary
has obstructed my way. The natural light of my childhood—
impossible to snare.
                                        Isn't it time I made my proclamations
and was gone?

Still, I so often want to rise to an everyday moment,
and if the canvas swallows me up,
                                                            I'll return
to fill the slow idea of sleep, "if not in body,
then in mind," and
                    the intolerable progress of all will reel
forward and rest.

                                        Of course the inscrutable
will beg the question, "How is it to be said?"

The genius of the place approaching
is as tangential as its means,
the odd diffuseness of the clocks
keeps finding me (though I'll never tell),

and the shore is only a dream
of how it got there, where that scheme of things
fits. Disciples have it wrong.
The pitch of things *seems* right, perhaps,
and with a little more close effort, someday I too
might have a star
to name.

So the descending line of variants still claims more
than it loots, and there's no shortage of departments
showing up like lines from the walls.

Now that the shrill dark distant
future is around, can we go home and be guests
someplace else?

I *can*
cough up everything, including the surroundings
of my life, which is not the mission it's confessed

to be,
            nor the thing warped calls
make marked confessions of.

There. I've claimed you. Now we
can go on.

THE REFUSAL

(2)

I continue to feed myself,
I risk losing stride. In the distance, truth
artfully just lost the game.
The time is almost right
for the distant, or near-distant past
to cling gratefully, once again, onto us
and handmaid us down
into the den of unmined pain
and fear we once knew, and knew at once.

If I sit here long enough one day
maybe the cactus will supplant my brief idea of it,
although I wouldn't want to rescue too much
from the mendicant world. Or I thought so once,
in another time, when culled laps of an eternal
roundabout grew, and godliness,
or virtue, whichever,
emerged from the internal.

Enough for now.
What's been swept inside the coffin
stays there,
until the structures of things come forth
to swallow it, and beauty begins to echo fear.

I keep urging things forward, almost
believing in power, or
its claim to stream from everything.

I have to shore against my ruins (for a while)
to be adequately scared.
I have to get out of bed. You all gather round.

By that time, you were off to another
shore, whose echo everyone knows, or is
at least familiar with, moved a little bit closer
to the lapsed idea of it.

Seems we could go on this way
in the casual life of things,

and the little lamps that gleam,
although they're just a pertinent reminder
to call home.

BECAUSE WE ARE MOVING

Still, we will want to go on moving

past the usual things, leave the light
of the last house behind, brush off our hats as we go,

tuck them into our coats. No one will see this.
No one will notice that we are moving

through cities and places, fields and events.
We will move on without each other

in mind, because it is in us to keep going.
Only the hills at the high-end will turn

and return as we pass through the towns,
round corners, trail through the dark, wheel

over things that have stopped. We will never stop.

Through that door—the cored frontier
came true. We, including the pasture,
hidden within. The wall of that far wall
inferred and narrowleaf where it
veered off.

Is there another sinking tune? Quicker,
more indelicate. Another viable lineage
that has lighted one's way.
The other life that wanted to be read.

FROM MEMORY

Then drew back across a field,
slow thin light rolling,
lifting now,

but only a handful of us to notice

the sun, swinging
grievously . . .

and you drawn
down
the fault lines

(what is leading us?)—

how spare
everything is, this is, is this all.

VI

MUTATIONS

audible
inhabited
in-
    ward
to rend

FINALLY I DECIDE TO CLOSE MYSELF TO LIGHT

One must relinquish all ideas of guardianship,

divorce oneself from seeing, prostrate oneself before darkness

A long and quiet flight   from the stir of dawn

AT THE DULL BORDER OF A CROWD

Abandoning her relation to (life), she declines into (life).

"The henchman has restored me, not my faith."

THE QUESTION STOOD BEFORE HER LIKE A TERRIBLE EYE

(You will not answer.)

AT ANY GIVEN MOMENT

There stands, as the object of my defiance, a cold and stolen hope that courses through the veins. *Slowly, achingly . . .*

. . . *On the brief floor of our pains, the profligate arrow falls.*

THE HARBORING OF ENDS

Each brief season, by degrees, is taken. We are, in this fashion, lost. Proceeding as such, we cannot help identifying with windows. That framed misery!

*

To retreat, and in doing so, to cut oneself spinewards. As if by emptying oneself into darkness, some transmission could occur.

*

That being said, I try to go outside, to castigate *outwards.*

*

Those whose entire claim is *I once was a handler of secrets and whims!* Bagh! I am waiting for the resurrection so I can hang myself on the trap of another life!

*

"In due time, the redemptive spirit will assert itself."

*

And each one deploring the living in my soul will mount up against my fear . . . and death (the specked dark and spurned ease of the last cutopen breath) will become another secret, named and taken!

THE NATURE OF BELIEF

I am in such a need of sun. There, on the surface of what was seemingly reliable, I fall

(Outside this morning, feel as though the long fracture of the mind has finally ripened)

Every angel falls and transposes her private doubt into a private excess of the soul

Exonerated, she climbs into unlife

VII

IN MIDAIR

"to taste, nameless, the nettling shade—"

AFTERWORD

After the fiction had peeled to one side,

After it was slit and laid into—

Sidelong, she peered.

And watched a deadlight on a captive ground.

The range of her confession

She would hang inside.

MEMORIES OF IMPERMANENCE

1

The story is recessed,
is
   wasting, now drawn away
from itself.
         Where you gesture backwards, looking . . .

2

You can easily see
the distance, now
                  ghastly,
aglow—
         the sun, intuitively, welled
up and returned to sight,
                  earth glaring.
         What would give way to
summit now, seeing
         there, some fairer
counterpart.
         You relinquish each
seeing with a
lie
         along bright paths,
you experience this as foundering.

3

We were trying
to see into.
Air, even at this pace,
moves into other
speeds.
In her—
seeing
hastened away
from, as if
filling out a distance,
budding into
likeness,
which, conceivably,
could miss everything.

4

Seeing resonates
through a distance.

A bird
flying off-
center, or in curves,
is this distance
slithering.

        Tracing it backwards,
you describe
        a young girl singing,
her impermanence
        at the moment of dawn.

5

        Or, a girl might turn away
in a moment of seeing,
        the dignity of her presence
opening into
        events.

        The event of her turning, for instance,
time extending
      backwards—

A space closes.

6

        A space outside her
extending . . .
        And gesturing widely there,
till backwards, blown,
                unhooks
a flower
        from ground . . .

7

She cannot understand
what is
leveling past.
In the same way
air is lightness,
does a bird signify
a crook or a fork in
thinking?
A fold or a bend in
tractable sky.

8

folding away
(expanding and folding),

two birds, one
of moderate size,
rippling through air
and
unraveling past us.

The other,
a blue vapor rising.

Where it thins
and
flees—

9

What is around her.

She pictures it now.

A figure is drawn
into water, it
resembles
the jostling
of leaves or of
flowers,
what she perceives
as leaf or as
a trace of—
folding away from
sight.

10

Nearing . . .
what is held in sight,
as a cloud lifts,

and a name
attaches itself to her through distance.

Just as air perceived as distance
allows her to sustain
a moment of seeing—

Lost moment of a dream,
stirring.

FIRELARME

After the disarrayed feeling

distraught, distracting, distracted,   sought

What she did, she grew to create herself. In the end, it was like a forest. Only the wood-keep was gone

Into the leaky den

He is fascinated by the stormdoor and the *firelarme* as he calls it. Also the watering trough and the bucket of ferns.

Her time here to be slated—
"Must come to be written, through the hedgehog and the bees."

It came to mean   there was something in the rafters, a woodchuck, or something

Would it be better to live in the forest, let the forest reclaim itself? Tame the woods

(so long as the invisible beckoned to her like fists—)

Was it not she at 1:00 A.M. shouting   I want to root *here*—

The lying one, the one bawling—through the window with terrible breath, the one with the cough that got worse, this one

who imagined her, who wrote her name backwards

This one
Returning
A name
Told through a slotted gate—

IN MIDAIR

slowing as
the air slows
everything
suspended
in its port

Each time I remember turning
endlessly in air—

Gone dry, the fretted branches
fluttering in pale light,

loose pebbles drowned
inside the river.

Death of leaf, of moth, of spring.
We tire, we tire endlessly.
A field of light redeems us

but only momentarily.

I remember saying, and this is what I said

come here and play me this measure.

Hours and no hours,
placid sun suspended

through morning air,
comprehension slips.

Branches that bleed, branches that bear lightly down,
I am the sun of placid suns,
phantom of birch leaves.

And trembling inside the river,
I drew my hands inside.

She looks around her, peers backwards.

jaundiced light
on a river that resembles
No river
in this—river of rocks
bloodwater
No thing fled
whither, bird

In the maniacal divide,
a bird appears hovering

In the divide,
a hovering bird

One yellow bird
now hovering in the wood—

"Little bird—
are you my
slashed
(intent)?"

A minaretted-heat

dragged
and
scattered
cross the
soft
cleated
earth.
Days
she tread, dead-
arm drawn under
like mutilated
birds.

---

the body's false chronology toiling in air that bird errant

a hand enters a hand stays she an alphabet undue light

smoke air smoke light how she wrought herself inside, idolatrous

circle unassailable

bereaved I traveled
        upward
        it was raining
        I felt
        things
        hostiling
        beside me
                everything scattered
                        a bird

                                full slot of sun
                                through its brain

---

                                        unbent I
                                        seemed a low
                                        bird
                                        flowers and rains
                                        in its mouth

Swept over the wall
with my lantern
I drew—a fist
first light
to whir
away

In the girl's mind, a shaking light, hands far at the wall
issuing,

hemmed in along the light

slipped past

into the end of the river

CONVERGENCES

first time she came to dust coming up, small horse stammering

i am beginning to count figures, she said, the air, a sequence of lines

(in order not to be tracked she speaks in signs—)

his hand on my stomach, she said what was the word for—

everything floating off between the trees, all by itself in branches, the landscape dripped into, or on

or so that's how i saw it, she said, how the sun rose, diurnally, upward, hands spooling wide

she laughed who's to prevent me from going off here—

from gradually slipping through lines, the landscape, into or on

the sky's several branches

and shall we bow to it? she said, turning their heads to

what she said was a sign, the sky a terrible hoar-cast, the air a locution

---

she wished   the air   would move
it touched her
fleeting
        border
she fired herself—

NEAR

            Burning on water, sound of
rain, moving quickly away from water, there is
                a sound like rain
on water. To be it would be to move quickly
into the rain, over the water, in-
to the sky's vanishing.

    Growing light,
                a rail of light
on water,
                a light
staining water, the way the eye
follows the stain back-
                wards in-
to its emptying
        out.

And moving
through trees,
    a shadow of a bird
—leaves.

---

receding into leaves a threadlight just before dissolving

bird withered river rock what she saw then slippery leaves

the leaves collapsing longer in their light their amphetamine glare

between rocks a slithering grammar

END OF DAY

The way the sky would play her thin out. To hold her name down like eaves coming down and swim blindingly through stars.

Until she couldn't tell which pattern she was counting. She was not counting now but shifting, crossing the patterns within her. Moving foolishly past.

By her own admission
the pathlight was suddenly
all gravelight.

Now again moving through the ongoing slate of
air again dropped
and then—abounding.

The sojourners hung cohorts, their laughter went out
in deranged meanings, clotted breaths, staid arrows of light

A rusted sun turned inward
and out, hid

and froze—

All that was flew riverward.

photo by Robin Rice

LISA LUBASCH was born in New Rochelle, New York in 1973. She grew up in Riverdale and on Long Island and currently lives in New York City. Her first book of poems, *How Many More of Them Are You?* (Avec Books, 1999), received the 2000 Norma Farber First Book Award.